TRANS FORMERS
ANIMATED

Transformers Animated: Bumblebee Versus Meltdown
Copyright © 2008 Hasbro. All Rights Reserved.
Printed in the United States of America.
No part of this book may be used or reproduced in any manner whatsoever without written
permission except in the case of brief quotations embodied in critical articles and reviews.
For information address HarperCollins Children's Books,
a division of HarperCollins Publishers,
1350 Avenue of the Americas, New York, NY 10019.
www.harpercollinschildrens.com

Library of Congress catalog card number: 2008920011
ISBN 978-0-06-088807-7
Book design by John Sazaklis
❖
First Edition

TRANSFORMERS
ANIMATED

Bumblebee
Versus
Meltdown

Adapted by
Aaron Rosenberg

Based on the episode *Total Meltdown*

HarperEntertainment
An Imprint of HarperCollins *Publishers*

On their new home, Earth, the Autobots continue to fight bad guys.
Bumblebee is the smallest, so sometimes he has trouble fighting by himself.
"Next time, find your foe's weakness," Prowl tells Bumblebee.

"If you can reach it!" Ratchet teases.

"Knock it off!" Bumblebee demands.

"Relax, little buddy," Bulkhead says.

"Why do you have to call me 'little'?" asks Bumblebee. He's upset.

Just then the Autobots get a call from their friend Dr. Isaac Sumdac. He's a scientist. "Help!" he cries. "Someone is breaking into my lab!"

"Autobots, roll out!" Optimus Prime orders. They all transform to vehicle mode and race to Sumdac's lab.

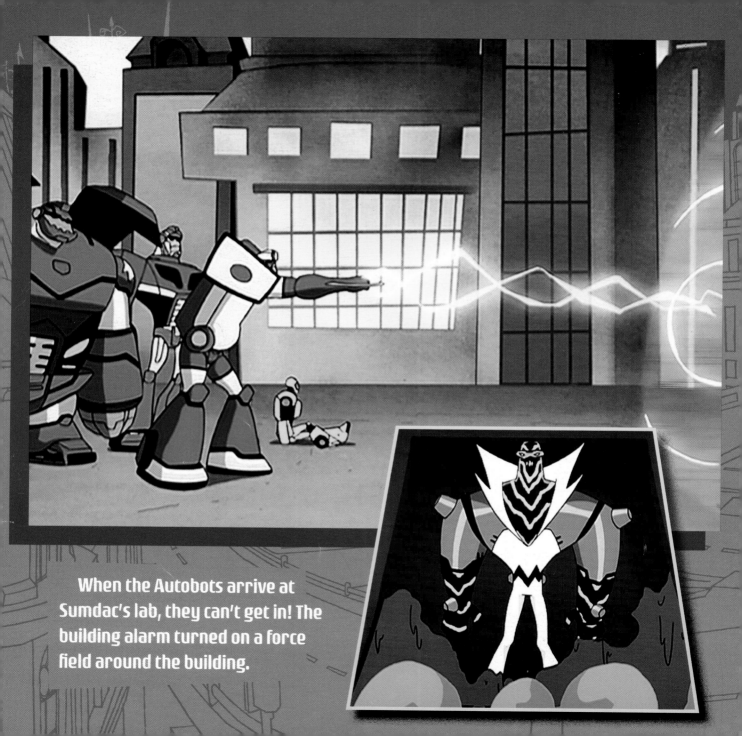

When the Autobots arrive at Sumdac's lab, they can't get in! The building alarm turned on a force field around the building.

"Hands off, machine!" says the bad guy.
Meltdown uses his acid to melt through Bulkhead's hand!

The big Autobot drops Meltdown. The villain prepares to fire more acid.

"No!" Bumblebee races to his friend's defense and dives in front of Bulkhead. Meltdown's acid hits Bumblebee instead.

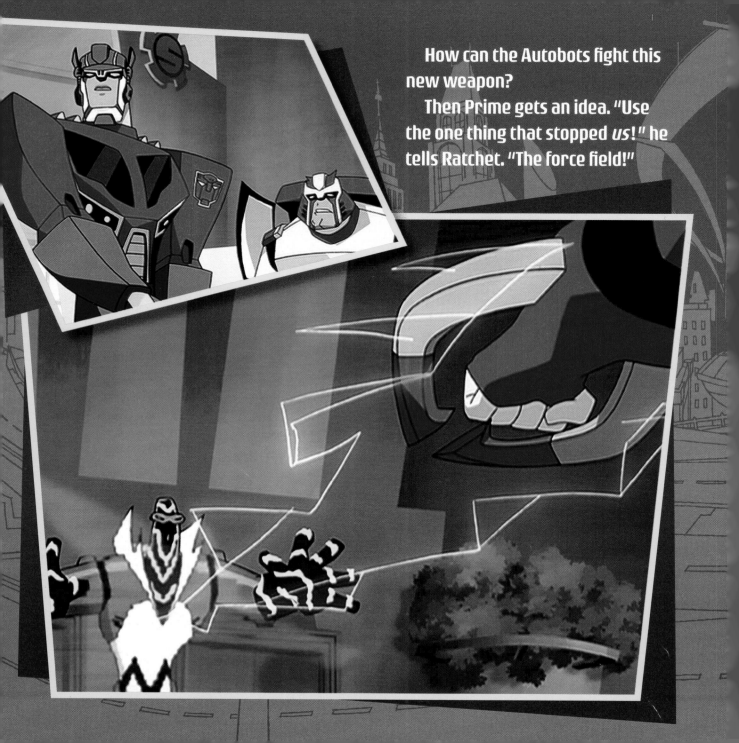

How can the Autobots fight this new weapon?

Then Prime gets an idea. "Use the one thing that stopped *us*!" he tells Ratchet. "The force field!"

Ratchet channels Sumdac's force field through his magnets. The force field traps Meltdown. He can't melt his way through that!

Bumblebee is the hero of the day!
"For a little bot, you've got a great, big spark," Ratchet says.
"You showed a lot of spark taking that hit for Bulkhead," Prime agrees.

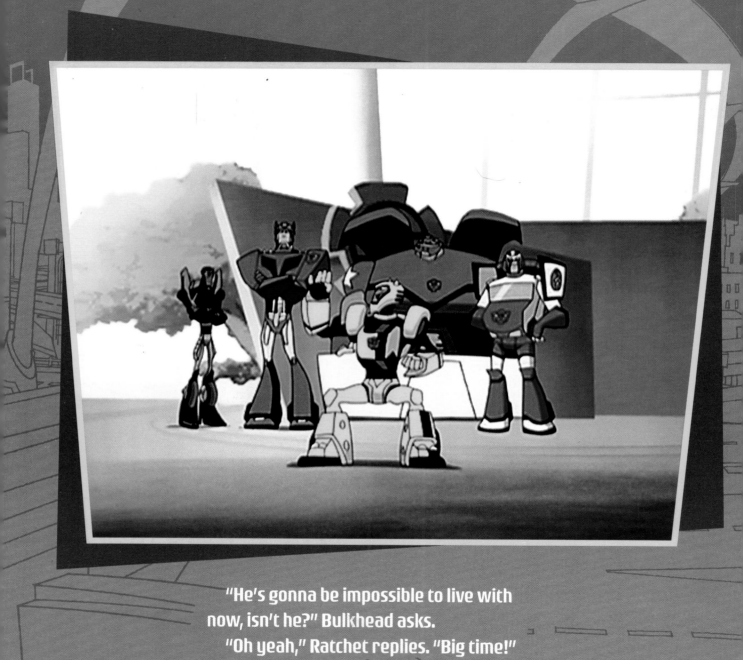

"He's gonna be impossible to live with now, isn't he?" Bulkhead asks.
"Oh yeah," Ratchet replies. "Big time!"